TWICE
TOLD
TALES

Twicetold Tales is published by Stone Arch Books
A Capstone Imprint
1710 Roe Crest Drive
North Mankato, Minnesota 56003
www.capstonepub.com

© 2014 Stone Arch Books

Library of Congress Cataloging-in-Publication Data
Snowe, Olivia.
  A home in the sky / by Olivia Snowe; illustrated by
Michelle Lamoreaux.
      p. cm. -- (Twicetold tales)
  Summary: In this modern version of Jack and the
beanstalk, Jack trades his bike for some magic beans,
and climbs the beanstalk to the apartment of Mr.
Briareus, a large man with a magic chicken and a
singing harp.
  ISBN 978-1-4342-5041-4 (library binding) -- ISBN
978-1-4342-6279-0 (paper over board)
1. Fairy tales. 2. Giants--Folklore. 3. Folklore--
England. [1. Fairy tales. 2. Giants--Folklore. 3. Folklore-
-England.] I. Lamoreaux, Michelle, ill. II. Jack and the
beanstalk. English. III. Title.
  PZ7.S41763Hom 2013
  398.20941--dc23
                              2013002778

Designer: Kay Fraser
Vector Images:: Shutterstock

Printed in the United States of America in
Stevens Point, Wisconsin.
032013   007227WZF13

A Home in the Sky

by Olivia Snowe

illustrated by Michelle Lamoreaux

STONE ARCH BOOKS™

You know the story.

You've heard it before.

Everyone has.

Now, read it again.

A new twist. A new gasp.

The story is told again.

TWICETOLD.

~1~

The boy on the bike, having dropped off the last of his newspapers, pedaled slowly up Farmhand Street. At the top, right before the railroad crossing, sat his apartment building, like a tired, stout, old lady made of deep-red bricks.

He pushed open the front door—the lock never worked—and carried his bike up three flights of stairs. He locked his bike to the railing before going inside.

He knew his lock wouldn't stop any thief for long. In this neighborhood, if someone wanted something, they took it—no matter who it belonged to.

"I'm home," he called into the dimly lit apartment.

His mother stuck her head out of the tiny kitchen. She was already dressed for work, though it wasn't yet six thirty in the morning.

"Hello, Jack," Mom said.

She ducked her head back in, and Jack went into the narrow kitchen and leaned on the counter.

Mom sipped her coffee and shuffled through envelopes and bills. Most of them, Jack noticed, were tinted red—those were the overdue ones.

"That doesn't look good," he said.

Mom sighed. "No," she admitted. "Jack, I'm sorry, but you're going to have give up this paper route. You're not making enough money doing that job."

"Huh?" Jack said. "Quit the paper route?" He pulled the orange juice from the fridge and poured himself a glass. Then he said, "Mom, I know it's not much money, but it's better than nothing."

He downed the OJ quickly. Then he smiled. "Oh, hey, I almost forgot," he said. He dug into the pocket of his faded, too-tight, too-short jeans and pulled out a crumpled-up pair of bills.

"Payday today," he said. He dropped the money on the counter. "Cha-ching!" he added, trying to make his mom laugh.

Mom smiled at him and pushed back his hair.

"Good job, Jack," she said, looking down

at the money. Then she sighed. "But honey, it's just not much."

"I know," Jack said, suddenly feeling hurt. "At least it's something, though."

"We'd make more by selling that bike of yours," she said.

Jack's jaw dropped. "Sell my bike? No way. You can't mean that," he said. "How will I get to school?"

"You can walk to school," Mom said. "Marie walks, doesn't she?"

Jack groaned. Marie, a seventh grader, lived up in Apartment 5B. Yeah, she walked to school. But it was a really long walk, and Marie always looked tired, and she never had good grades.

"It's a really long walk, Mom," Jack said. "I wouldn't have time to do anything. Like homework."

"I'm sorry, dear," Mom said. "But I don't

know what else we can do." She checked her watch. "I have to get to work," she added. "I can't be late."

She put her empty coffee cup in the sink and grabbed her bag. "After school today, please start looking for a buyer for the bike," she said. "I'm sure one of those bike shops downtown would be happy to give you . . . oh, say fifty dollars for it?"

"Ha!" Jack said. "Fifty bucks?"

The bike was worth a lot more than fifty dollars. He'd won it in a raffle held by the newspaper. He'd only bought one ticket, but it was the one that counted.

"It would really help us out," Mom said from the apartment doorway. "Now you get off to school, okay?"

The door slammed and Jack rested his head on the kitchen counter. It was cold and smelled like a wet, dirty rag.

"Whatever," he muttered.

Mom shouted from the hallway through the closed door: "Things will get better soon! You'll see!"

Jack groaned. "Yeah, right."

2

Jack didn't bother going home after school. Instead, he went downtown on his bike, straight to his favorite bike shop, Slim's.

"Why the long face, killer?" Slim said when Jack pushed his bike through the shop's front door. "Bike trouble?"

Slim was a big guy—fat, despite the nickname. He was always sweaty, from being in the shop's back room doing repairs. His hands were thick and covered with grease more often than not. Slim wiped off a wrench—looked like a fifteen millimeter—and slipped it into the back pocket of his overalls.

"The worst kind of bike trouble," Jack said. He leaned his bike against the shop's counter. "Mom's making me sell it."

Slim's eyes went wide. "What?" he said. "That's horrible. I'm sickened."

"Me too," Jack said. "But I guess we need the money worse than I need a bike—or a paper route."

Slim shook his head slowly and clucked his tongue. "So, what are you going to do?" he asked.

"That's why I'm here," Jack said. "Wanna buy it?"

Slim's face fell. "I can't help you, killer," he said. "I don't buy used bikes."

"Aw," Jack said. "Why not?"

Slim picked up a black binder from the counter. He flipped through the pages and then turned it to face Jack.

"How do we know it's not stolen?" Slim said, pointing at the open page. It was a list of bikes, by color and size and style and brand, that had been reported missing.

"Come on," Jack said, grinning. "Seriously? It's me! You've repaired this bike for me a dozen times."

"But the police don't know that," Slim said. He stepped back from the counter. "It's the same at every shop, all over town. Ask anyone you like."

"So you won't buy any used bikes?" Jack asked. "That's that?"

Slim shook his head. "It's way too much of a risk for me," he said. "One stolen bike sold, and I could lose my whole business." He looked at Jack's bike and smiled. "Sure wish I could," he added. "Your bike is a great one."

"I know," Jack said sadly. "You sure you can't make an exception?"

Slim sighed. "No can do," he said. With that, Slim disappeared into the back room. "Sorry, killer!" he called out.

"It's okay," Jack mumbled.

Jack rolled his bike back outside. There were a few other bike stores nearby. He figured it would be a long afternoon.

～3～

By five o'clock, Jack had been in every bike shop in town.

As it turned out, Slim was right. No one would buy a used bike because used bikes were often stolen bikes. At the last shop, Jack finally asked, "If you don't buy used bikes, how come you all sell used bikes?"

"Some people," the last shop's owner said, "donate their bikes." Then he got up from the counter to help a customer.

Donate their bikes? Jack thought. *That's insane.*

Jack rolled his bike outside. He figured if he couldn't sell it, at least he'd get to keep it. That thought cheered him up, and he hopped onto his bike to ride home.

He'd just started through the alley behind the only skyscraper in town when someone called out to him.

"Hey, kid!" a dry and raspy voice said. "That's a great bike. Is it for sale?"

~4~

Jack squeezed the brake lever hard. His rear wheel came around, squealing, and he skidded to a stop. He looked around frantically, but there was no one around.

"I'm right here," said the voice. And right in front of Jack—how could he have missed him?—was an old and bent man dressed in clothes so dirty and ragged that it was impossible to say where the coat ended and the pants began.

In fact, Jack thought as he got a closer look, he couldn't be sure this man wasn't dressed in something like an old canvas robe or gown— something a wizard would wear in a children's fairy tale.

"You want to buy my bike?" Jack said as he hopped down from the seat. As he got closer, he gagged a little.

The man smelled. He smelled of the street and of sweat and of smoke and oil and gasoline, like most people who live on the street. But this man had another scent, too— spicy, earthy, and foreign.

The old man nodded several times, very slowly. His grin was wise, wide, and toothy, and his teeth were bright and sharp.

"Because you don't look like a big bicyclist," Jack said.

The man ignored the comments and started digging through his pockets, taking out random items. He pulled out scraps of paper, some metal toys, a banana, two apples, a cooked chicken leg . . . but no money.

"My mom wants me to get at least five hundred dollars for this," Jack said. He was sure this weird old guy wouldn't find that in those ragged pockets.

"You want money, eh?" the man said. He was short, Jack realized, and the man looked up at him with the expectant and mischievous smile of an ill-behaved toddler. "I can give you money."

"Great!" said Jack.

"I can make you rich beyond your wildest dreams!" the man went on.

"Wait, what?" Jack said. This guy seemed crazier by the second. And those teeth were kind of scary, like bared fangs on a rabid dog.

Jack started to back away. "Listen, never mind," he said. "I think I'll keep the bike."

"Wait!" the man snapped, and he snatched

for Jack's wrist. His hand was quick—so quick that Jack hardly saw it move. It was more like a blur, and then it was around Jack's wrist, hard—painful.

"Let me go," Jack said. He tugged and tugged, but the little man's grip was a vise.

It was just a moment—just the briefest instant—but the man sneered wickedly, his face darkening and his eyes flashing red. Then, as if it had never happened, the man released Jack's wrist and put up his hands.

A grin spread across his face like wings. "I mean no harm," he said. "Simply, do not run off just yet."

"Okay," Jack said, rubbing his wrist. "Ow."

The man bowed, and, staying stooped over, clasped his hands together as if to beg. "You think me crazy?"

Jack shrugged. "No . . ." he said. His voice was tentative and shaky.

"You do," the man said, nodding quickly. "Oh, you do. I've seen it so many times. But look!"

He reached into his pocket again. This time he didn't search wildly or pull out loads of junk and garbage. He knew just what he was grabbing.

"Magic," the man said, and now his voice was deep and rich. He held up a tiny bag made of shining, golden fabric. The bag was cinched at the very top with a narrow cord of black thread.

Jack took the bag. He opened the top and turned it out into his hand. From the bag tumbled a half dozen brown and pale gray . . .

"Beans," Jack said. "They're beans."

The man's grin grew wider still. His eyes were shining and bright as he looked up at Jack.

"They can be yours," the old man whispered, as if someone would desperately want a handful of beans, "along with all the magic they possess. All you have to do is give me the bike."

Jack almost laughed. "Come on," he said. "What do you think this is? A fairy tale?" And he looked directly into the man's shining eyes, and the man reached out again—more gently this time, almost carefully—and took Jack's wrist in his hand.

"The magic is real," he said, and now his smile vanished. His voice became quiet and heavy, like it came not from his body, but from somewhere deep in the Earth itself. "It only remains to be seen whether you will take the chance and grab it."

Jack's mouth opened—he meant to speak. He meant to say no, or to laugh, or to pull his hand away and ride home as fast as his legs would take him.

But instead he said, "Riches?"

The man nodded. His grin, with its rabid-dog teeth, returned.

"Riches," he repeated. "Beyond your wildest dreams."

And then it was done. Jack's hand closed around the beans, and the man led the bike away.

~5~

"What?" Jack's mom shouted. "Beans?"

"Mom," Jack said. He looked at the beans on the little table in their makeshift dining room. "They're magic."

He could hardly bring himself to believe it anymore.

Why had he been so stupid?

Mom put a hand on her hip and stared at her son.

"I'm sorry," he said, letting his chin fall to his chest. "I think he hypnotized me or something."

She took a deep breath and sighed. "Just bring them back," she said. "Find this magician, give him his stupid beans, and get your bike back. It's worth more than beans, I'm sure."

"I can't do that," Jack protested. "We traded fair and square." Besides, Jack thought without even meaning to, they might be magic.

"You just said he hypnotized you," his mom replied. "That doesn't sound very fair to me."

Jack groaned and rolled his eyes. "That's not the point," he said, even though it was the point. Why couldn't he shake the feeling that he had to keep those beans?

"Where'd you even find this guy?" she asked as she pulled him up by the elbow. "Now go."

"Right now?" he said.

"Were you planning to wait till this man was a hundred miles away?" Mom asked.

She opened the apartment door and practically shoved her son down the hall.

"Go!" she snapped, and she slammed the door.

To Jack's surprise, when he went back to the alley behind the skyscraper, the wizened old weirdo was still there. He was sitting on the ground, leaning against a big, blue recycling tub.

"Hey!" Jack said as he jogged over. "Am I glad I found you. Listen, my mom is pretty upset with me."

"Is she?" the man said.

"Yeah," Jack said. "And to be honest, I don't know what I was thinking giving you my bike for a bunch of silly beans."

He dug into his pocket and pulled out the beans. "So here they are," he said, holding out his hand.

Jack stared down at the beans. He couldn't take his eyes off them.

Stop it, he ordered himself. *They're just beans.*

Jack blinked hard and shook his head to clear it. "You can have them back and I'll take the bike back," he said, reaching them toward the little man again.

The man laughed. "I'm afraid I can't do that," he said.

"Why not?" Jack said. "Come on. Here's the beans."

"It would be impossible," the man said.

"Why?" Jack asked.

"I'm afraid I already ate your bike," the man said. He climbed to his feet, groaning the whole way up from the dirty ground.

"Ate it?" Jack said. "Boy, you are crazy, aren't you?"

The man cackled and coughed. He put up one finger, as if telling Jack to wait, and then disappeared around the far side of the recycling tub.

"Good," Jack said to himself. He shook the beans in his loose fist, thinking the man would be back at any moment with his bike. "He sure has a weird sense of humor, though."

After nearly a minute, the man still hadn't reappeared. "Hey," Jack called, peeking around the recycling tub. "What are you up to—?"

But the man was gone.

Jack looked down at the beans in his hand. "Well," he muttered, "Mom's going to kill me."

With that, he headed out of the alley. He

found that the beans grew warm as he walked. Soon, they were uncomfortably hot in the palm of his hand.

"Ow," he muttered, and without thinking, he tossed the beans over a brick wall as he walked.

~7~

M om was furious when Jack showed up
at home with no bike and no beans.

Jack tried over and over to explain that he
was sorry, and that this man was definitely
crazy. He admitted time and again that it was
his fault, but Mom just wasn't satisfied.

The next day was Saturday, and in the
morning—before seven o'clock—his mom
woke him up. "Get dressed," she said.

"What? No school today. No more paper route," Jack protested.

"Time to find a better job," Mom said. "A job that pays more than a couple of bucks every two weeks."

"Now?" Jack said. "No one's even open yet."

"Diners are open," Mom said. "And delis. And they need dishwashers."

Jack sat up on the couch—it doubled as his bed these days, since he and Mom had moved into the tiny apartment.

He rubbed his face to help himself wake up. "Okay," he muttered. "I'm awake."

The streets of Jack's little city were empty. Mom was right—the diners were all open, and so were the doughnut shop and the bagel store and the coffee shop. But they all had dishwashers already. They let him fill out an application, but it was pretty obvious to Jack that he'd never hear back from them.

By eleven, he'd written his name and address and relevant experience (that is, none) on about ten different forms. And he was hungry.

He was about to head home when he spotted—like a bright-red streak of lightning—his bike.

"Hey!" he shouted, and he took off running. "Stop!"

It was the little odd man, zooming around downtown. As he zipped and flew down the empty streets and sidewalks, he laughed and hollered: "Can't catch me, Magic Jack! Can't catch me!"

"Come back, you crazy old—" Jack shouted. He tore down streets and alleys. Every time he turned a corner, the bike zipped by and was out of sight.

Finally Jack was back at the alley behind the skyscraper. But the bike, it seemed, had vanished for good. Jack didn't see it—or the crazy old man—anywhere.

And after running for so long and so fast,

Jack was exhausted. He sat down against a fence and wiped the sweat from his forehead and the back of his neck.

"That's funny," he said to himself, staring at the thick-trunked, bright-green tree across the alley from where he sat. "I don't remember that tree being there yesterday."

He shaded his eyes and squinted up at the tree, higher and higher. It twisted and turned as it climbed, so high that he couldn't see the top of it. It seemed to be as tall as the skyscraper it grew behind—maybe even taller. And all the way up, it was green and smooth, with lots of vines and big, broad leaves growing out of it, instead of rough and brown and covered with bark, like a tree should be.

Jack climbed to his feet and walked across the alley. "I don't think this is a tree," he mumbled. Closer to the tree, he saw that the vines, which climbed all around the big plant and the fence and even onto the skyscraper

itself, bore little pea pods. Jack pulled one off
and tore it open.

Bright-green beans tumbled to the
pavement. Jack smiled. These were his beans.
This was his beanstalk.

Magic, he thought.

Then he started climbing.

Jack climbed. He seemed to climb for hours, but it was never difficult. It was warm, and a cooling breeze pushed him from behind, as if to help him climb.

As he went, he sometimes picked a pod of beans—he ate a handful, and shoved some in his pockets. After all, they were really magic, weren't they?

Now and then, Jack could see into the skyscraper beside the huge beanstalk. Most of the floors were offices, with men and women hunched over desks, or walking sternly down lushly carpeted hallways, all well dressed in dark suits and all serious-looking, with set jaws and no smiles.

None of the people glanced out the huge windows. No one seemed to notice the sinewy, bright-green stalk that had sprung up overnight beside the tower. None of the people—so distracted and busy and committed to their tasks—saw the boy climbing, only feet from their desks.

On other floors were apartments, most with drawn blinds and lights off, their residents no doubt at work — maybe at the offices right there in the same skyscraper.

That would be something, Jack thought as he climbed. *To live and work right there in the same building.*

He wondered if there was a school inside this skyscraper too, and hairstylists and restaurants and grocery stores. Maybe these people simply never went outside.

And it was then, when he'd almost forgotten he'd been climbing, that Jack reached the top of the beanstalk.

The narrowing plant startled him from his thoughts and he looked down.

The world spun around him. The wind picked up, and he hugged the stalk for dear life. Dark clouds moved in from the southwest. The air was cold and seemed to sing with electricity. It would storm any second, Jack knew.

"What am I doing?" he shouted to himself against the sound of the approaching storm. It was as if all the magic of the beanstalk and his long and easy climb suddenly fell away. He realized at once that he was in great danger, a thousand feet above the hard pavement of his little city.

Jack searched desperately. Below him, about twenty feet down, jutting out from the top floor of the huge building, was a covered balcony. As lightning cracked across the darkening sky, Jack knew he had no choice but to climb down to that balcony to find cover.

The stalk was slippery now. He clawed at its sides to hold on. The skinny vines that tangled up and around the stalk clung to his legs, as if trying to stop him or trying to trip him.

Jack tugged free of the vines and, half sliding and half climbing, made it to the balcony.

He jumped from the stalk and landed in a crumpled heap on the balcony floor. At the same instant, the sky opened with rain—a torrential downpour.

Jack hurried farther under the balcony's roof. He huddled against the big glass doors that led into the apartment beyond.

When lightning cracked again, Jack turned, desperate for a safe, dry place. The glass door was open, just a little bit. It slid easily all the way open and Jack, still crawling, hurried inside. He closed the door behind him, silencing the storm.

Jack leaned against the inside of the glass door and stared at the room he'd found himself in.

It was like nothing he'd ever seen, outside of movies and TV shows. The furniture was covered in soft-looking, dark leather. Framed paintings hung from the walls. A big wooden desk boasted small sculptures and golden trinkets. Hanging on the wall facing the desk was a huge flatscreen TV.

"Wow," Jack said. "Whoever lives here must be the richest person in town." He was righter

than he knew. But for now, these riches—at least, the ones he could see from where he huddled against the glass doors—were his for the taking.

He could take any of them and become rich.

All it would take would be putting one in his pocket.

Jack shook the thought away. He wasn't a thief, after all. He was a hardworking kid with a paper route and good grades. He hoped to move out of his neighborhood, but for now, just because he lived among so many thieves didn't mean he had to be one himself.

But this is magic, Jack thought.

Here, in the safety of the apartment, the storm that had sent him fleeing inside seemed miles away.

From where he sat, he could see fancy crystal pieces, expensive electronics, jewelry, and even an egg made of pure gold.

Any one of those things—stuffed into his pockets and down the beanstalk with him— would pay his mom's debts, and probably keep them above water for months.

Those things could change their lives.

"This is the magic," Jack whispered into the dark apartment. "This is it. Not the beans. The beanstalk was just the doorway up here, really. But the crazy old man was right. I found riches beyond my wildest dreams."

Jack got to his feet and moved toward the big wooden desk. "Besides," he said, "these people are so rich, they wouldn't even notice if something was missing."

He was about to grab the golden egg from its resting place when he spotted a box. It was smaller than a loaf of bread, trimmed in leather and mother of pearl.

Jack flipped up the top and caught his breath. Inside were dozens of shining gold coins.

"Real treasure," he said in a quiet, worshipful voice.

Then he reached in, grabbed handfuls, and shoved the coins into his pockets.

As he reached for the golden egg again, something thumped in the hallway. Footsteps grew louder and faster.

Someone was coming.

~11~

With his pockets heavy and jingling, Jack ran for the sliding door. He threw it open and, not bothering to close it behind him, was across the balcony in two long strides. He leaped over the railing and grabbed hold of the beanstalk.

As he slid and twisted among the vines and bean pods on the giant stalk, Jack squinted through the rain and gloom at the glass door. He could just make out a figure—a huge figure—stomping through the room.

The huge man stood in the middle of the room, sniffing the air, as if he might pick up the scent of a thief from the broke-down apartment building at the top of Farmhand Street. But through the rain and dark, he couldn't see Jack outside; Jack could tell.

But he might at any moment, Jack thought, so Jack climbed and slid down as fast as he could.

~12~

Jack slammed into the apartment, the smile on his face as big as the whole outdoors. He ran into the kitchen, shoved past his mom, and turned his pockets out onto the counter.

"Ta-da!" he said.

Mom's jaw fell open. Her face went white and she brought her hand to her mouth.

"Wh—" she started. "Wha—"

Jack laughed and threw his arms around her. He held her by the shoulders, grinning. "We're set, Mom," he said. "No more debt. No more dumpy apartment."

"Where did you get these?" Mom said. She wriggled from his hug and ran her fingers over and through the piles of gold.

"I found them," Jack said, but his mom could hardly hear him—she was barely listening. Instead she sorted through the piles of coins, trying to guess the value of this treasure.

Without another word, Mom grabbed a paper sack from under the kitchen sink. She slid the coins into the bag, folded the top, and grabbed her coat. She shoved the bag into her coat's big pocket.

"Let's go," she said.

"Go?" Jack said, hurrying to keep up as his mom slipped out the apartment door. "Where?"

Mom was already a flight down the steps.

"Don't you plan to lock the door?" Jack shouted.

"Why?" she called up to him. "To protect our worthless junk? We have riches, right here in my pocket!"

Smiling, Jack jumped down the steps, two at a time.

~13~

On the north edge of town was a small, curious shop. Hardly anyone went in, but everyone who passed it wondered about it: what could there be in there? How does the crazy shopkeeper stay open, if no one ever buys anything?

The window display was so cluttered that one couldn't see into the store, but one could see a collection of the oddest things imaginable: copper-headed horse dolls, antique cuckoo clocks, thick books bound in leather and edged in gold, and all manner of contraption that no one other than the shopkeeper herself could identify.

But such a bunch of clutter was intimidating to most of the people in and around town. So no one ever went in—and most of the townspeople assumed that's how the shopkeeper liked it: quiet, dusty, cluttered, and empty of strangers.

When Jack and his mom pushed through the heavy front door—its glass opaque with years of grime—and set the bell to jingling, the shopkeeper behind the counter at the back of the store nearly fell from her stool.

"What do you want?" the shopkeeper said. She found her glasses atop a pile of junk on the high counter in front of her and slipped them over her hooked nose.

On her stool, she looked rather like a

ragged and tired old vulture. "The shop is closed!" she said.

"The sign says you're open," Jack pointed out. "Besides, the door was unlocked."

"Ah, well . . ." the woman said. She pulled off her glasses and rubbed her eyes. "Very well. Don't touch anything."

"We're not here to shop," Jack's mom said. She stepped forward and dropped the paper bag on the counter. At the jangly sound of the coins, the shopkeeper's eyes went wide, as did her grin.

"Selling?" she said. "Very good. Very good." Eagerly, she opened the bag and reached in. She pulled out handful after handful of gold coins until the bag was empty and the coins were in neat piles in front of her.

"A nice collection," she whispered. "A very nice collection."

Then she looked up at Jack. "In my experience, a person doesn't come across such a collection by accident," she said, peering at him.

"What's that supposed to mean?" Jack asked, frowning.

The old woman looked at him with her eyes narrow. "I think you know," she whispered.

Her gaze seemed to burn—was it more magic?

Or was it guilt?

Nonsense, Jack told himself.

We need this money.

I don't feel guilty at all.

In a flash, the shopkeeper's face went bright again. She grinned and said, "It's a fine collection. I can pay you well—if you wish to part with it."

"Of course we do," Jack's mom said, smiling gently at the shopkeeper. "That's why we're here."

"Very well," the shopkeeper said, and she hopped down from her stool.

To Jack's surprise, off the stool she was shorter than he was—only a few feet tall. She hobbled into a back room and came back with a checkbook as big as she was. Then she climbed back up the stool, pulled out a check, and, with her big feather pen, hunched over the checkbook and filled it out in big flamboyant writing. "There you are," the woman said. "Take it or leave it."

"How much?" Jack said, trying to get a look over his mom's shoulder. But she folded it and tucked it away.

"Thank you," Mom said. She stayed composed, but Jack could tell that inside she was ecstatic.

"Have a good day," the shopkeeper said as she came down from her stool. She hurried around the counter and pushed them toward the door. "We're closing right now. Good-bye."

In a moment, Jack and his mom were on the sidewalk outside. The door slammed behind them, and bolt after bolt slid home.

"She's weird," Jack said.

"Jack," his mom said, reaching into her bag. "My dear, sweet son. Look at this."

She held out the check.

"It can't be right," Jack said. "It can't be."

It was more money than Jack had ever seen in his life.

"Our problems are solved, Jack," Mom said. "We're out of the woods."

~14~

The check changed their lives. Mom paid all their overdue bills. She caught up on their rent. The check was so large, in fact, that Mom was able to pay up the remainder of their lease on the apartment and buy them a small house in a nicer part of town. She quit two of her jobs.

Everything was great.

But Jack still wasn't happy. He wanted his bike back.

It was a long shot, but it was summer now and Jack didn't have anywhere he needed to be. So one morning, after his mom headed to work, Jack got dressed and started walking.

Their new house, which was two stories and light blue with white trim, sat on a beautiful green lawn, with shrubs and a single fat-trunked ancient maple tree in the center of the backyard. It sat among hundreds of other two-story houses, some light blue like Jack's, others white or pale gray or canary yellow or soft green.

The neighborhood squatted around the lake on the east side of the city, as far from Farmhand Street as a person could get. The walk to the skyscraper downtown would take an hour or more.

Jack didn't mind. He knew he probably wouldn't find the old man who bought his bike. But if he did, maybe the man would sell it back.

After all, Jack definitely had enough money to buy it.

And if the man wasn't there—well, Jack had a few other ideas about what he might do with his morning. Maybe he'd go back up to the palace in the sky.

Nah, Jack thought as he walked toward downtown, thinking of the beanstalk to the clouds. It's probably been cut down by now.

But it hadn't been. Several blocks from the skyscraper, Jack spotted it. The passersby—and there were many—ignored it.

Maybe that's part of its magic, Jack thought. *Maybe only I notice it, because I know to look for it. Because it's mine.*

Jack moved through the sea of weekday people—some were shoppers, some were workers, some seemed to have nowhere in particular to be.

Not one of them seemed to notice the beanstalk that climbed over a thousand feet into the sky.

Jack slipped into the alley behind the skyscraper and there, at the base of his giant plant, was the odd old man—the man who traded him the magic beans.

And he was sitting atop Jack's old bike.

"Jack's back!" the old man said. He cackled, and one of his eyes twitched and winked madly.

"I want my bike back," Jack said. He dug into his pocket and pulled out a thick wad of cash. "I can pay you way more than it's worth."

That just seemed to make the old man laugh even more. He nearly fell off the bike. "This bike," he said, crying with laughter, "is not for sale."

So suddenly that Jack flinched, the man stopped laughing and his face became quite serious.

"Why don't you climb again?" the man whispered. "Climb again and steal some more, Jack the Thief."

Jack shoved his money back in his pocket— worried, just for an instant, that someone might see it.

"It's not stealing," he said. "It's magic."

The man laughed and laughed. He rode off, still laughing, and called over his shoulder as he rode away: "Yes, it's magic, Magic Jack. It's magic!" His laughter echoed through the alley as he vanished.

~15~

"Forget that weird old man," Jack said to himself. "I will climb again. I'll find enough riches up there to buy a hundred bikes—the best bikes in the world, too!"

And climb he did.

No storms came. No wind threatened to pull Jack from the beanstalk and send him tumbling to the ground and his demise. This time it was easy. He climbed all the way up to the top.

Then he hopped down lightly from the giant plant, onto the safety of the terrace, and once again the sliding door was ajar.

Jack slipped inside. The big living room's lights were off, and the next door, which led to the rest of the palatial apartment, stood open. The hall lights, too, were off.

No one home? Jack thought. *It can't hurt to have a look around—see what else this millionaire might have.*

Jack sniffed the air. Something smelled great—the scent of freshly baked desserts wafted into the living room. Jack couldn't help but follow the smell. Maybe the millionaire had left something delicious sitting out. Or his housekeeper had.

Jack tiptoed down the hall. Every door he passed stood open, just a little bit, and every light in every room was off. He made his way to the kitchen and gently pushed open the swinging door.

"Whoa," he said. Even though they had moved—even with his new house, with their new kitchen and his own bedroom and the family room in the basement—Jack was blown away by this apartment's kitchen.

The counters were huge and high and made of slabs of black stone. The refrigerator and stove gleamed as if they were covered in gold. Huge windows on the far wall let in the bright noon sunlight.

Jack squinted against the light and spotted a plate of doughnuts on the big island in the center of the kitchen.

"Ah!" he said, and he grabbed two at once. "I knew I smelled something." In seconds, his mouth was full and his face was powdered with confectioner's sugar.

He stood in the middle of the huge kitchen, licking the sugar from his fingertips. They were the best doughnuts he'd ever had. In fact, he might have forgotten why he was in this magical, millionaire kitchen. He might have found a bag, filled it with the rest of the doughnuts, and left.

But then something clucked.

~16~

Jack stopped, frozen, with one finger in his mouth.

It clucked again.

"Hello?" he said, though he was certain he'd heard a chicken, and a chicken probably wouldn't respond to "hello."

Cluck!

Jack spun and found the source of the cluck: a cupboard with a big door, in its center a wire screen—like an old-fashioned pie cabinet. But this cabinet definitely didn't contain pies.

Jack moved carefully across the kitchen as he finished licking the sugar from his fingers. He bent down.

The cabinet was near the tiled floor, under the heavy slab counters. Jack peered through the screen. It was dark in there. He could just make out a vague, white shape.

Cluck! Cluckcluckcluck!

Jack yelped and jumped back. Inside the closed cabinet, the chicken flapped and clucked madly.

"Shh!" Jack said, hurrying back to the screen. "Good chicken."

But the chicken wouldn't be calmed. It clucked and squawked and flapped and hopped around.

"Please!" Jack said. "Be quiet!" He tried the cabinet door, but it wouldn't budge. And that made the chicken cluck even louder and flail even wilder.

I have to let it out, Jack thought. *It's probably scared to death.*

Jack pulled open the kitchen drawers. He found towels and plastic wrap and wooden spoons. There seemed to be a hundred drawers, but finally he found something that might work.

He pulled out a big ladle—made of heavy metal—and ran back to the cabinet. The chicken was insane by this point, flapping its wings and clucking its head off.

Jack wedged the big spoon's handle into the cabinet door. He pulled and tugged, and the door cracked open, just a tiny bit—but it was enough to jam in the whole spoon and really give it a tug.

With a great snap, the door flew off. It fell to the tile floor, clattering loudly.

The chicken followed the door, clucking

and flapping its wings, bouncing around the kitchen.

It snapped its beak at Jack. It hopped onto the counter, sending the doughnuts and their plate crashing to the floor. The plate shattered into a hundred pieces.

"Shush!" Jack said. He chased the chicken around the kitchen. He dove for it, his arms out in a hug, and he missed. He tried again and again.

Finally he got close—he came away with two handfuls of soft white feathers that the chicken had shed—but he dove straight into the empty chicken cabinet.

With his head inside, he could see the chicken's nest and the eggs inside it. They were sort of yellow, he realized, not like any chicken eggs he'd ever seen.

He grabbed one as he struggled to back up out of the cabinet—and it nearly dropped it right away.

It wasn't warm, like a fresh egg ought to be. It was quite cold—and quite heavy.

Jack pulled himself out of the cabinet and, on his knees, grabbed an egg in each hand.

They were both very, very cold. They were both very, very heavy—much heavier than two eggs from a chicken ought to be.

He stood up, holding the two eggs, and, as he watched the chicken pecking around the kitchen, he realized something.

The golden egg in the living room.

That was no jeweler's creation.

It came from this nest.

That chicken laid eggs made of pure gold.

"No wonder this person is so rich," Jack said. "He has a constant supply of gold."

If Jack had a chicken like this one, he'd have as many bikes as he wanted. His mom would have a kitchen like this one. She could quit her job. They could travel the world. He wouldn't need school, or college—he wouldn't need anything, ever!

His grin grew to a huge smile.

"Come here, cute little magic chicken," Jack said.

He moved slowly toward the chicken. It was much calmer now.

Jack stayed low to the ground. As he crawled toward the bird, he scooped up a chunk of the fallen doughnuts. He held it out to the bird. Surely even a chicken would love a sugary treat.

It worked. The chicken, hesitant at first, strutted toward Jack. It pecked at the crumbs in his hand. It hurt a little; the little beak was sharp. But Jack knew it would be worth the pain.

As the chicken snapped up bit after bit of doughnut, Jack suddenly threw his arms around the fat bird's body. He quickly clamped one hand over its beak, stood up, and ran from the kitchen.

Halfway down the hall, Jack skidded to a stop. At the far end of the hall, the apartment's front door was opening.

~17~

For an instant, Jack stood there, frozen, staring at the wide-open front doorway and the giant man it framed. He had to stoop to fit through the door. His shoulders barely squeezed through. If this giant got his hands on Jack, it would be the end of him.

"You!" shouted the man in the doorway. He sniffed, and he sniffed again. He squinted and twisted his mouth, as if thinking and struggling to recall something.

Then his eyes went wide and he bellowed, balling his hands into huge fists: "You stole my coins!"

Jack, barely able to breathe, found the open door to the living room. He hurried through and leaped over the couch. Behind him, the giant stomped down the hall. But big as he was, he wasn't fast, and Jack was on the terrace before the giant was in the room.

"See ya!" Jack said. He cradled the chicken under one arm like a football and leaped to the beanstalk.

"You can't escape!" the huge man called after him, his voice booming like thunder.

But Jack did escape. He slid and climbed quickly down the beanstalk, its top hidden in the clouds, and the huge man at the top never knew where Jack had disappeared to.

★ ★ ★

"A chicken?" Jack's mom said. "Jack, what do we want with a chicken?"

Jack dug in his pockets. He pulled out two, three, four eggs and put them on the table. They rolled and wobbled.

"What is this, Jack?" his mom asked. She picked one up.

"It's gold," Jack said.

"Gold," she whispered. She smiled. She picked up the other eggs and said louder: "Gold." She looked at Jack. Their eyes met, and they both smiled happily.

Then, in a flash, the smile was gone. Mom held up the egg and snapped at Jack, "Where did you get this . . . thing?" She pointed at the hen under his arm. "Tell me the truth, Jack. Right now."

And finally, after so many months of

wealth, and the newfound everlasting riches that could come from the hen, Jack told his mom everything.

He told her about the weird old man.

He told her how the beans had sprouted and grown into a ladder that reached up to the sky.

And he told her about the palatial apartment at the top of the skyscraper.

After Jack's tale, Mom sat down in a dining room chair. She didn't say anything. Jack waited, but for minutes, she didn't speak.

She stared at her reflection in the golden egg in her hand, and then she stared at another of the eggs that sat on the dining table in front of her.

"Mom," Jack said, sitting down next to her. "I can see you're upset. You think I'm a thief. But it's not like that. It's magic. Don't you see? The magic got us all this stuff. You've worked so hard, and now you won't have to anymore."

"No," Mom said. She shook her head. "You stole this stuff. We stole this stuff!"

She put down the egg and stood up. "Show me," she said. "Show me the beanstalk."

~18~

They took Mom's car downtown. They parked in front of the skyscraper. Even though they were rich, they didn't have any change for the meter.

Too bad the parking meter doesn't take golden eggs, Jack thought.

"Don't worry, Mom," Jack said, hurrying her along. "We can afford a parking ticket."

Mom sighed, but she followed him down the alley without paying for their parking spot.

At the base of the big plant, Jack stopped and put his hands on his hips and smiled.

Mom's face went white. "This is it?" she asked. "And it goes all the way to the top? You're sure?"

Jack nodded.

"I know who lives there," Mom said.

Jack gasped. "You do?" he asked. "Who lives there?"

"That's the penthouse apartment of Don Briareus," Mom said, her voice hushed and afraid.

"Who's that?" Jack asked.

"He's the most powerful man in town— one of the richest and most powerful men in the world," Mom explained. She took a deep breath. "Jack, that man owns half of the whole city. He owns the apartment building where we used to live—and most of the rest of Farmhand Street, probably."

"But Mom," Jack said. "He's rich because of that silly chicken. He's rich from magic too!"

"No," Mom said. "We can't let this continue. We have to give everything back. The house. The coins. The gold eggs. Everything. He'll find us. He'll make us pay."

"He doesn't sound very nice," Jack said, looking at his feet.

"Nice isn't the issue," Mom said, and she grabbed Jack by the hand. "Come on. We're going upstairs."

"What?!" Jack said. "No way, Mom. We can't do that."

But his mom dragged him around to the front of the building, right into the lobby, and up to the security desk.

"We've been expecting you," the guard said as he stood up. He leaned both hands on his desk. His mouth twisted into a satisfied and unpleasant smile. "You can go right up."

"Thank you," Jack's mom said. "But first—" She reached into her purse and pulled out a dollar bill. "Do you have change for the parking meter?"

~19~

On the hundredth story of the building, Jack and his mom stepped out of the leather-lined, golden elevator. The floor was covered with a thick, lush, red carpet.

"Wow," Mom whispered.

A single huge white door stood before them. On it, rather than a number, was a name in shining gold letters: BRIAREUS.

"I guess we should knock?" Mom said. She stepped forward and raised her first, but before she could strike, the door swung open.

The hallway was completely unfamiliar to Jack. All the lights were on, and it made the long hall seem welcoming—inviting, even.

Jack and his mom moved slowly down the hallway. It had been years since Jack held his mom's hand, but now he did.

All the doors along the hall were closed tight—except one. They stopped in front of the open door, about halfway down the hall, and looked in.

There, sitting on a big leather couch, was Mr. Briareus. When he saw them, he smiled and stood up.

Though Jack had seen him before—had fled from him—as Mr. Briareus stood to his full height, Jack and his mother both gasped at the enormity of the man.

"Welcome to my home," he said. "Please,

come into my office and take a seat." He waved at two chairs facing the big couch.

"Thank you," Mom said. "We're so sorry about all this."

Mr. Briareus nodded and ushered them toward the chairs.

Jack's mom did her best to smile, but she was still afraid—Jack could tell. Who wouldn't be afraid of this man? He was powerful not just financially and politically, but physically. If he wanted, Jack realized, Mr. Briareus could crush the two of them in one hand.

Jack refused to smile, but he sat down in the chair next to his mom's and crossed his arms.

"Do you have something to say to me, little man?" said Mr. Briareus through his toothy smile.

"No," Jack snapped back.

"Jack!" his mom whispered harshly. "Apologize. Confess!"

But Jack didn't answer. He didn't apologize or confess. He didn't nod or shake his head. He just grunted once and refolded his arms across his chest.

The big man laughed. "It doesn't matter, miss," he said. "You and I—and your boy—all know what he did. And we all know exactly how much he's stolen from me."

Mom shifted in her seat. "Oh, dear," she muttered.

"You're right to be nervous," Mr. Briareus said, giving a short, angry laugh.

He strode across the hardwood office floor, stepped around to the far side of his desk, and sat down in his big desk chair.

With his back to the window, a shadow fell across Mr. Briareus's face so that Jack couldn't see it. But Jack was sure the giant's smile was gone.

"Today," the man said, "I am your arresting police officer. I am your judge, your jury, and your prosecutor. And today, I find you both guilty of theft."

He leaned forward and pushed a button on the desk. Before Jack or his mom could move, straps shot up from the floor and the arms of their chairs.

They were trapped.

"And," Mr. Briareus said, "I sentence you to life imprisonment."

~20~

The giant dragged Mom's chair out of the room as she struggled against her bonds.

"I'll be back to deal with you in a moment," Briareus said.

"Help me, Jack!" Mom cried.

But Jack couldn't budge from his chair, no matter how hard he struggled.

"Mom!" he shouted as Briareus pulled her through the office door. "Let her go! She didn't do anything!"

But his shouting was in vain. The office door slammed behind them. Jack heard a key in the door, and the click of a lock.

"Mom!" he shouted once more, but no one answered.

Desperately, Jack looked around the room for anything that might help him escape from this chair and this room before Briareus got back.

He shuffled his chair, and it scraped loudly. He smiled a little, thinking of the nasty scuff marks it would leave on the perfect wood floors. At home, his mom would ground him for that.

Quickly, Jack scraped and hopped his chair toward the low cabinet along one wall. Jack pulled open every door and scanned every shelf.

There were books and little sculptures and an antique harp and other useless junk. None of it would help Jack escape.

Jack paused a moment and strained to hear even the slightest sound in the hallway.

Silence.

Wherever that giant had taken his mom, it was taking a while to get back.

He slid his chair toward the big desk, then shimmied so one arm was against the front of the desk, and he grabbed the drawer.

Locked.

But atop the desk, right in the middle, was a letter opener— it looked like a plain, symmetrical knife.

It might work, if I could reach it, Jack thought. But he couldn't reach it. He had to knock it to within reach.

With a great grunt of effort, Jack slammed his chair into the desk, giving it a good shake.

The letter opener hopped a few inches. He slammed into the desk again, and the opener moved some more.

He was making a huge racket, but it was working. He had to keep trying.

One more great thump, and the desk scraped loudly on the floor. The letter opener leaped into the air and skidded across the big desktop, all the way to the edge. It teetered, and then it fell with a clang.

Jack hurried, scraping and hopping madly. Then he took a deep breath, closed his eyes, and pushed himself over.

He landed with a heavy thud, his head knocking on the wood, ringing like a coconut. But he could reach. He grabbed the letter opener and began scraping its sharp edge against the bonds on his wrist.

It was hard work, but soon he heard the bonds ripping and pulling away. His hand was free.

Getting the other three bonds was much easier, and soon, with the letter opener in hand, Jack was free.

He ran for the door, but stopped.

Someone was singing. Right there in the office, he heard music and singing—it was the most beautiful thing he'd ever heard.

~21~

But he hadn't seen a radio. *A radio?* Jack thought.

He'd only seen the harp.

There it was. He noticed now that the harp was golden, and its frame was shaped kind of like a woman in a dress. And the woman's arms were plucking the strings.

And the woman was singing.

"Amazing," Jack whispered, and the harp stopped playing.

"Don't stop!" he said quickly, because it was the most beautiful music he'd ever heard, and she was the most beautiful woman he'd ever seen. "Please, keep playing."

She smiled at him. He stood right beside her now.

"I am only supposed to play for the master," she said in a voice that sounded like crystal, and Jack thought for a moment that he would cry, because he'd never hear that song again.

"You sang for me just now," he said.

"I shouldn't have," the harp said. "The master would be angry."

And then Jack did cry. He didn't want to But he cried, more than he had in years and years.

Still, the harp wouldn't play.

Jack could think of nothing else, though, because the harp, of course, was magic, too.

"You should not stay here," she said.

"Why?" Jack said through his tears. "Where else would I ever want to be?" He could not imagine being away from this harp. Even if she wouldn't play, he'd rather be close to her, just in case she decided to play again someday.

He pleaded, "Please. Play for me one more time."

"You must help your mother," she said. Her voice was not only beautiful—it was sad, a sadness so deep and profound that Jack could hardly listen to her without crying again.

But the word "mother" seemed to snap something in his mind. He remembered where he was and what he was doing and what he had to do: find his mother and get her out of this mad giant's apartment.

"You're right," he said. "But what about you?"

"Me?" the harp said.

"You're a prisoner here too, aren't you?" Jack said.

"Something like that," the harp said. "Will you help me leave too?"

"I will," Jack said, and he grabbed the harp. "But you have to help me first."

~22~

J ack popped the office door open with his letter opener. He stuck his head into the hallway and spotted Briareus leaving the living room and locking the door behind him.

"Here he comes," Jack said. "You know what to do?"

The harp smiled and nodded, and Jack put her down on the thick, red hallway carpeting, just outside the office door.

Then he ducked back inside, leaving the door open the tiniest crack. He stood at the door and waited.

He didn't have to wait long.

"What are you doing out here?" the giant shouted. His footsteps thundered down the hall as he ran toward the harp. "Did that little thief get away?"

But the harp didn't answer. Instead, she began to play. It was her finest song, and her voice was more pure and beautiful than even Mr. Briareus had ever heard it before.

By the time he reached the harp, he was slow, calm, and happy. He began weeping tears of joy that flowed down his cheeks and over his grin like a salty waterfall.

Jack risked a peek through the crack in the door. Briareus picked up the harp and held it against his chest. She looked tiny against his huge frame. The tears still streamed down his face, and he smiled with his eyes closed.

Now was Jack's chance. As quiet as he could, he slipped out the office door and ran down the long hallway, thanking his stars that the thick carpeting muted his footsteps.

At the living room door, he picked the lock and hurried inside. "Mom!" he said. There she was, still bound in her chair.

"Oh, Jack," she said. "Thank goodness. He's insane!"

"I know," Jack said, nodding. He bent down and started to cut the straps that held her to the chair.

"We have to hurry," he said. "We can climb down the beanstalk."

"What?" she said. She rubbed her wrists and stood up. "Why don't we go out the front?"

Jack pulled her to the hallway. There was Mr. Briareus, between them and the front door. They waited and watched until he went into the office.

"Go out on the terrace," Jack said. "I'll be right there."

"Where are you going?" Mom asked.

"I made a promise I have to keep," he said. "Just go."

Jack closed the living room door and ran back to the office. He stopped just outside the door and peeked inside. The harp spotted him. It was her cue to stop playing and singing. She stopped, and the silence in the office, after her magical song, filled Jack's chest with sorrow and pain. But he pushed through it. He had to, if they were to escape.

The giant, though, sat on the big leather couch with his head in his hands, and he sobbed. "Why won't you play?" he said through his hiccups and tears.

But the harp would not, and the giant just sobbed and sobbed. His great shoulders bucked and he hiccupped and coughed like a toddler having tantrum.

Jack tiptoed across the wood floor. He put his hands gently on the harp and turned to leave. Everything was working perfectly.

"Please . . ." the giant said.

Jack was almost out of the office.

The giant lifted his tear-stained face to plead once more. "Play—" he started to say. Then he jumped to his feet. "You!"

~23~

J ack ran. He tore down the long hallway, nearly past the closed living room door. He slammed into it shoulder first, not bothering with the doorknob. "Come on, Mom," he said without stopping. "We have to go now. Seriously, come on, hurry up."

With the harp against his chest and belly, he ran across the room, hurdled over a couch, and launched himself off the terrace, right onto the beanstalk.

Mom stayed close behind. Soon they were both on their way down.

The magic was with them, and the climb was fast. But above them, Mr. Briareus climbed too. The beanstalk swayed under the giant's weight.

"You won't escape, little thieves," he shouted down at them.

When Jack and his mom reached the safety of the pavement, he handed her the harp.

"Mom, this is Harp," he said. "She's . . . magic."

The harp smiled.

"I'll be right back," Jack said, and he ran to the front of the building.

Inside, the guard jumped to his feet. "How did you get down here?" he said.

But Jack ignored him. He ran to a glass door marked FIRE, and he closed his eyes and smashed the door with his elbow.

Inside, he found an ax.

"Whew," he said to himself as he ran from the lobby. "If there'd just been a hose and no ax, I'd be in trouble."

He ran back to the beanstalk. "Step back, Mom," he said, and he swung the ax.

Thwack!

He swung it again.

Thwack!

He swung it again.

Thwack!

Again.

Thwack!

Again.

Thwack!

One more big swing, and he was clean through the beanstalk.

Then he waited.

Like a great, ancient tree, the beanstalk

leaned slowly, and then faster and faster and faster it toppled, bringing Mr. Briareus down with it.

The beanstalk fell, and the giant landed on the pavement blocks and blocks away.

~24~

Months later, Jack biked through his new neighborhood. From the bag on his back came beautiful music, and though no one stopped him to ask what it was, all who heard it knew—way down deep—that it was magic.

He pulled his bike into the garage and leaned it against the wall. In the house, he found his mother sitting in the easy chair in the living room, reading. He pulled Harp from his bag and set her on the table by the window, where she liked it best.

Mom looked up and smiled at both of them, and Harp began to sing.

Harp had told Jack everything—about Mr. Briareus, and how he'd come to have his riches. (It was not by being nice, or by being savvy in business. He was a crook and a killer.) And Harp had explained more about the magic beans and the odd old man.

It had all been magic, Harp said, and Jack would never go hungry again.

Jack sat down on the couch and put his feet up. He closed his eyes and just listened.

Jack and the Beanstalk

• ★ • ★ •

Jack and the Beanstalk is an English fairy tale that's at least two hundred years old. No one knows exactly when the story was written, but a version first appeared in print in 1807.

In the original tale, Jack lives with his mother, who is a widow. Jack's mother sends him to the marketplace to sell their cow, which has stopped producing milk. But on the way to the market, Jack meets an old man who offers him magic beans in exchange for the cow.

Jack accepts this trade, which makes his mother furious. She tosses the beans out the window. But as they sleep that night, the beans grow into a huge beanstalk that stretches into the clouds.

When Jack climbs the beanstalk, he finds that it leads to a house in the sky. The house is home to a giant and his wife. Jack begs for food from the wife, but he must hide from the giant, who eats humans. The giant's wife helps him to hide, and as Jack escapes, he finds—and takes—a bag of gold coins.

The second time Jack climbs up to the giant's house, he steals a hen that lays golden eggs. And the third time, he takes a harp that can play music on its own. But as he leaves, he's almost caught by the giant, and he must use his ax to cut down the beanstalk. This kills the giant, and Jack and his mother live happily—and richly—ever after.

Tell your own twicetold tale!

• ★ • ★ •

Choose one from each group, and write a story that combines all of the elements you've chosen.

A girl who doesn't know she's a princess

A prince whose mother has just died

A young woman who is lost in the woods

A boy who lives alone in a city

A rose	A castle
An orange	A mansion
A pocket of silver	A hut in a forest
A glass cup	A ship at sea

A newborn baby	A dog
A goblin	A cat
An angry witch	A chicken
A sad emperor	A goat

Los Angeles
Ancient Rome
An English village
India

More
Twicetold
Tales

TWICE TOLD TALES

Cassie and the Woolf
by Olivia Snowe

TWICE TOLD TALES

The Sealed-Up House
by Olivia Snowe

TWICE TOLD TALES

by Olivia Snowe

The Girl and the Seven Thieves

about the author

Olivia Snowe lives between the falls, the forest, and the creek in Minneapolis, Minnesota.

about the illustrator

Michelle Lamoreaux was born and raised in Utah. She studied at Southern Utah University and graduated with a BFA in Illustration. She likes working with both digital and traditional media. She currently lives and works in Cedar City, Utah.